Millions of Americans remember Dick and Jane (and Sally and Spot too!). The little stories with their simple vocabulary words and warmly rendered illustrations were a hallmark of American education in the 1950s and 1960s.

But the first Dick and Jane stories actually appeared much earlier—in the Scott Foresman Elson Basic Reader Pre-Primer, copyright 1930. These books featured short, upbeat, and highly readable stories for children. The pages were filled with colorful characters and large, easy-to-read Century Schoolbook typeface. There were fun adventures around every corner of Dick and Jane's world.

Generations of American children learned to read with Dick and Jane, and many still cherish the memory of reading the simple stories on their own. Today, Pearson Scott Foresman remains committed to helping all children learn to read—and love to read. As part of Pearson Education, the world's largest educational publisher, Pearson Scott Foresman is honored to reissue these classic Dick and Jane stories, with Grosset & Dunlap, a division of Penguin Young Readers Group. Reading has always been at the heart of everything we do, and we sincerely hope that reading is an important part of your life too.

GROSSET & DUNLAP
Published by the Penguin Group
Penguin Group (USA) Inc., 375 Hudson Street, New York, New York 10014, U.S.A.
Penguin Group (Canada), 10 Alcorn Avenue, Toronto, Ontario, Canada M4V 3B2
(a division of Pearson Penguin Canada Inc.)
Penguin Books Ltd, 80 Strand, London WC2R 0RL, England
Penguin Ireland, 25 St Stephen's Green, Dublin 2, Ireland
(a division of Penguin Books Ltd)
Penguin Group (Australia), 250 Camberwell Road, Camberwell, Victoria 3124, Australia
(a division of Pearson Australia Group Pty Ltd)
Penguin Books India Pvt Ltd, 11 Community Centre, Panchsheel Park,
New Delhi - 110 017, India
Penguin Group (NZ), Cnr Airborne and Rosedale Roads, Albany, Auckland 1310, New Zealand
(a division of Pearson New Zealand Ltd)
Penguin Books (South Africa) (Pty) Ltd, 24 Sturdee Avenue, Rosebank,
Johannesburg 2196, South Africa

Penguin Books Ltd, Registered Offices:
80 Strand, London WC2R 0RL, England

Dick and Jane is a registered trademark of Addison-Wesley Educational Publishers, Inc.
From THE NEW FUN WITH DICK AND JANE. Copyright © 1956 by Scott, Foresman and
Company, copyright renewed 1984. From FUN WITH DICK AND JANE. Copyright © 1940
by Scott, Foresman and Company. All rights reserved. Published in 2004 by Grosset & Dunlap,
a division of Penguin Young Readers Group, 345 Hudson Street, New York, NY, 10014.
GROSSET & DUNLAP is a trademark of Penguin Group (USA) Inc.
Published simultaneously in Canada. Printed in the U.S.A.

The Library of Congress has catalogued the original edition as follows:

Fun with Dick and Jane.
p. cm. — (Read with Dick and Jane)
Summary: A collection of classic Dick and Jane stories in which they
play with Sally, Tim, Spot, Puff, and their parents.
ISBN 0-448-43411-3
[1. Play—Fiction. 2. Pets—Fiction. 3. Vocabulary.] I. Series.
PZ7.F96615 2004
[E]—dc22
2003016832

12 13 14 15 16 17 18 19 20

Dick and Jane

E
Di

Fun With
Dick and Jane

Grosset & Dunlap • New York

Table of Contents

Look Up

Dick said, "Look, look.

Look up.

Look up, up, up."

Jane said, "Run, run.
Run, Dick, run.
Run and see."

"Look, look," said Dick.

"See Sally.

See funny Sally and Father."

"See, see," said Sally.

"Sally is up, up, up.

This is fun for Sally."

Who Is It?

Dick said, "Who is here?
Who is it, Mother?"

Mother said, "It is Dick."

"Oh, Mother," said Dick.
"You can see who it is."

"Who is this?" said Father.
"Who is it?"

Mother said, "It is not Dick.
It is not Jane.
It is not little Baby Sally.
It is big, big Father."

"Yes, yes," said Baby Sally.
"Oh, Mother, you can see."

Jane said, "Who is here?
Who is it, Mother?"

"It is not Dick," said Mother.
"It is not Jane."

"Not Jane," said Sally.
"Oh, oh! This is fun."

"It is Sally," said Mother.

"Yes, Mother," said Dick.
"It is little Baby Sally.
Funny little Sally."

"See my family," said Mother.
"My funny, funny family is here."

"Spot is here," said Dick.
"And Puff is here.
See this big, big family."

Something Pretty

Mother said, "Look, look.
See this."

"Oh, oh," said Sally.
"It is pretty."

"Yes, yes," said Jane.
"Mother looks pretty."

"Look, Sally," said Jane.

"Here is something pretty.

Something pretty for you and me."

"Oh, Jane," said Sally.

"I want something.

I want something red.

I want something blue."

"I want this," said Jane.

"And this and this.

Three for me.

Three for you.

Something yellow.

Something red.

Something blue."

"Look, Mother," said Sally.
"Red, yellow, blue!"

"Look, Mother," said Jane.
"We look pretty."

"Oh, yes," said Mother.
"Yes, Jane, yes!
You look pretty.
Sally looks pretty, too."

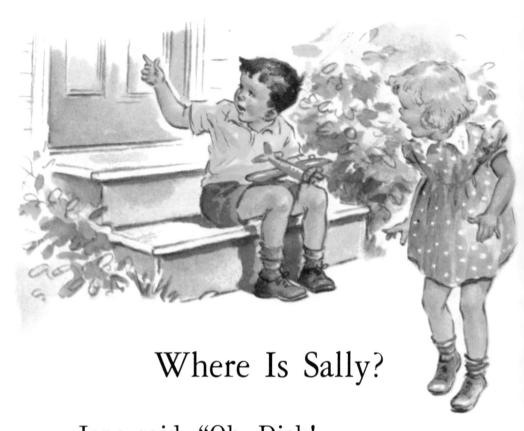

Where Is Sally?

Jane said, "Oh, Dick!
I can not find Sally.
Where is Sally?
Help me, Dick.
Help me find Sally."

Dick said, "Look in the house.
You will find Sally in the house."

"Look, Jane," said Dick.
"Here is something funny.
Can you guess what it is?"

"Oh, yes," said Jane.
"I can guess.
I can guess what it is.
This will help me find Sally."

Dick said, "Look here, Jane.
Look and see what I see."

"I see," said Jane.
"I see what you see.
I can guess where Sally is.
Now I can find Sally."

"Oh, Sally," said Dick.

"Here you are.

Now I see you.

I see Puff, too.

My, my! Puff looks funny."

Sally said, "Puff looks pretty.

Puff is not yellow now.

Puff is pretty.

See pretty, pretty Puff."

Jane Helps Mother

"I can work," said Dick.
"I can help Mother."

Jane said, "I can work, too.
I can help.
Look, Dick.
This is for Father.
Father will eat here."

Jane said, "One, two, three, four.

One is for Father.

One is for Mother.

One is for Dick.

And one is Baby Sally's.

One, two, three, four.

One for Father.

One for Mother.

One for Dick.

And one for Baby Sally."

Jane said, "Look, Dick.
You will eat here."

"Oh, Jane," said Dick.
"Where will you eat?"

"Oh, my," said Sally.
"Where will Jane eat?"

Jane said, "One, two, three, four.
I see four in this family.
Father, Mother, Dick, and Sally.
Father is one.
Mother is two.
Dick is three.
Sally is four.
One, two, three, four."

Dick said, "Oh, Jane!
You are funny.
You are in this family, too.
Where will you eat?
Where is one for you?
Now get one for Jane."

"Oh, oh," said Jane.
"Now I will get one for me.
Here it is.
This one is for me."

A Funny Ride

Father said, "I want something.
I want to get something.
Something for the car.
We can get it here."

"Oh, Father," said Sally.
"What do you want?
What do you want for the car?"

Father said, "You will see.
You will see."

Up, up went the car.

"Oh, oh," said Jane.

"See the car go up.

The car can go for a ride.

It can ride up."

Sally said, "Oh! See Tim!

He went up, too.

He and Spot and Puff went up."

Sally said, "Look, Father!
Spot and Puff want to jump.
Please make the car come down.
Can you make it come down?"

"Yes, Sally," said Father.
"We can make the car come down.
We will get Spot and Puff and Tim."

"Look, Sally," said Dick.
"See the car come down.
See Tim come down.
See Spot and Puff come down."

Sally said, "Down comes the car.
Down comes Spot.
Down comes Puff.
And down comes Tim."

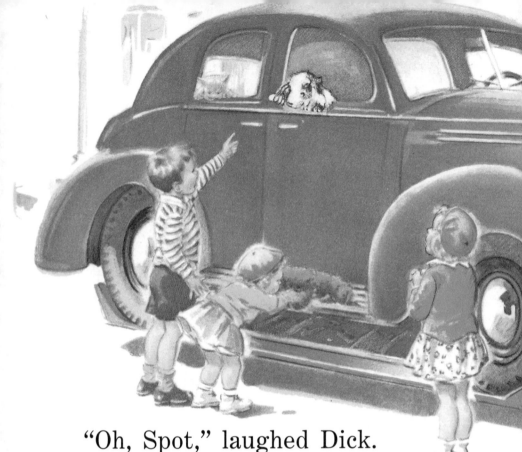

"Oh, Spot," laughed Dick.

"You ride up.

You ride down.

You ride up and down.

This is a funny ride for you.

A funny ride for you.

A funny ride for Puff.

And a funny ride for Tim."

Father went to the car.

He said, "The car can go.

The family can go.

The family can go away."

"Away we go," said Sally.

"We will not ride up and down.

We will ride away."

Away went the car.

Away went the family.

Away, away, away.

E

Dick

Fun with Dick and
Jane.

6/11

BEGINNER READER

DATE			